D0606237

The Legend of King Arthur

A Young Reader's Edition of the Classic Story by Howard Pyle

Illustrated by Luigi Galante, Simone Boni, and Francesca D'Ottavi
Retold by David Borgenicht

COURAGE BOOKS
AN IMPRINT OF RUNNING PRESS
PHILADELPHIA • LONDON

9 8 7 6 5 4 3 2 1
Digit on the right indicates the number of this printing.

ISBN 1–56138–503–4
Library of Congress Cataloging-in-Publication Number 94–74315

Cover and interior illustrations by Luigi Galante, Simone Boni, and Francesca D'Ottavi
Edited by William King and Elaine M. Bucher
Printed and bound in China

Published by Courage Books, an imprint of
Running Press Book Publishers
125 South Twenty-second Street
Philadelphia, Pennsylvania 19103–4399

Contents

Introduction

Within these pages is a new version of an oft-told tale, the Legend of King Arthur. It is the story of prophecies, plots, and battles, of youth, ambition, innocence, and truth—the tale of a young prince who is taken from the castle as a mere infant, and who finds his way to the British crown many years later with the help of fate, a magnificent sword, and magic.

This story of King Arthur has its origins in the history and lore of the ancient British people, the Celts. In the sixth century lived a renowned Celtic leader named Arthur. Literature recalls the existence of an even earlier, mythical Arthur, possibly a Celtic god, and it is this Arthur who has made his way into the hearts and minds of centuries of readers.

The Celts told and retold the story of Arthur, attempting to produce a coherent tale out of many sources. After nearly a thousand years of retellings, the Arthurian legends were given a permanent form in Sir Thomas Malory's *Le Morte d'Arthur (The Death of Arthur)*.

From this master storyteller's tale of great romance and intrigue, the most recent versions have come. Alfred, Lord Tennyson retold the legend in *The Idylls of the King* (1859–1885). Mark Twain lampooned the legend in *A Connecticut Yankee in King Arthur's Court* in 1889, and T. H. White brought a modern evocative tone to the tale in his 1958 masterwork, *The Once and Future King*.

This retelling is based on *The Story of King Arthur and his Knights*, first published in 1903 by Howard Pyle, the distinguished American artist and writer.

Here is the story of King Arthur and the sword in the stone, retold just for young readers, and for all who believe in valiance, honor, and the power of magic.

The Ancient Days

In the ancient days, when knights fought valiantly and sorcerers worked their dark and wondrous magic, an extraordinary child was born to the king and queen of Britain.

The king was the wise and noble Uther-Pendragon, and the queen the gentle and independent Igraine. They loved their newborn son with all their hearts and souls, and took great pride in playing with him, even though ruling all of Britain was quite a task.

The child was watched protectively by the mysterious royal sage: Merlin the Wise, who was a powerful enchanter and foreseer. Merlin believed that the child was destined for greatness.

The prince was named Arthur, and he was a wonder. He was strong and beautiful, with eyes that seemed to hold the very sky within them. He could crawl about before most children could hold up their heads, and could even lift his father's scepter high. As he looked about the world around him, Arthur appeared to understand who and where he was—even when he plodded along awkwardly behind his mother's gown, the new prince seemed to hold himself royally.

When Arthur was but six months old, Merlin awoke in his bedchamber with a shiver. Now, no one knew exactly how old Merlin was; some said two hundred years. Others said Merlin had seen the pyramids being built. Whatever his actual age, Merlin was certainly old, and old people often have shivers.

But the shiver Merlin had that morning was of a different kind.

A prophesy had come to him while he slept—a dark vision that foretold of bad things to come for the royal family. He had to tell the king and queen immediately. Merlin got up, threw on his enchanter's cloak, and left his tower in search of the king and queen.

He found them in the throne room with the prince. "My lord," Merlin said as he bowed, "My lady," as he bowed again, "I have dreamt of the future, and it is not good." Merlin's deep voice filled the room, and Igraine stopped rocking Arthur.

"I am sorry to say, sire, but very soon, you will fall gravely ill. It will begin as a strong fever, and will only worsen as time passes. I am not certain *how* you will die exactly, but I am certain that you will die."

Uther-Pendragon took his wife's hand, and Arthur stirred in his cradle. Merlin paced the room as he continued.

"When this happens, the kingdom will fall victim to chaos, and the prince's life will be in danger. Many of your old enemies, long quiet, will rise up and attempt to claim the throne for themselves.

"There is nothing we can do to stop this," Merlin answered before the king and queen could ask, "but we can protect the child. Allow me to hide Arthur until he reaches manhood. I will see that he remains safe from the evil that will overcome the kingdom."

The room was cold and silent while the king and queen thought about Merlin's prophesy.

Finally, Uther-Pendragon breathed deeply, and spoke with calmness and courage. "I have never known your visions to be wrong, Merlin, though I wish at this moment that I had. As far as my death is concerned, when my time comes, I will be ready to greet it. But my young son is not yet ready for death.

"It grieves me to think of him apart from his mother and me. But he must remain safe to rule one day." Uther-Pendragon looked into the queen's eyes, and they nodded silent agreement—they knew what had to be done.

"Take him away tomorrow night, under cover of darkness," spoke the King. "And take care of him—we will miss him."

Merlin simply bowed and left the room.

And so late the next night, Merlin went to the young prince's room, placed him in a basket, covered him with an old, torn blanket, and left the castle.

As Merlin predicted, the king passed away two weeks later of a strange sickness, and the kingdom fell into disorder. For eighteen years, lords fought amongst each other for their manors. Cruel knights and vicious barons pillaged and destroyed small hamlets. Wicked cutthroats and thieves prowled the roads, robbing and killing travelers.

Chaos reigned over the empty throne.

Even the church could not keep order. The Archbishop of Canterbury, the highest church official in the land, was at his wits' end. True, he was a notorious worrier. It had been said that the Archbishop's bedchamber floor was once replaced because it had been worn down from so much pacing.

But this time the Archbishop was worried for good reason. He had tried everything in his power to calm the people and restore order, and nothing had worked. Finally, he sent a messenger to summon Merlin for advice.

Merlin came promptly. The Archbishop was awaiting Merlin in his chamber, frantically rubbing his hands, and he breathed a loud sigh of relief when Merlin entered.

"Merlin, thank you for coming," the Archbishop said, vigorously shaking Merlin's hand and leading him to sit down.

"You are the wisest man in the kingdom," he said. Merlin raised his thick, gray eyebrows, but did not disagree. "Can you not find a way to calm and soothe this woeful kingdom? Since the death of Uther-Pendragon, we have known only strife. What can we do to restore happiness?"

"We need only wait, your worship," Merlin said. "I have foreseen that this country will soon have another king. This king will restore peace, and will be greater and more worthy of praise than even Uther-Pendragon. Moreover, he will be of Uther-Pendragon's own royal blood."

The Archbishop's face grew bright. "This is wonderful news, Merlin! Wonderful, wonderful! But when will the new king come? And how will we know him? Many lords and knights want to claim the throne—how will we know the real king when he arrives?"

"If I have your worship's permission," explained Merlin, "I will create a test that can only be passed by the true king. When he who is worthy

passes the test, all the world will know that he is the rightful heir to the throne."

"If it will restore peace to this war-torn kingdom," said the Archbishop, "you may do whatever it takes."

Merlin arose, left the cathedral, and stopped in the square outside. The sky was a dim pink-gray from the smoke of burning castles. Merlin raised his arms aloft, and began his sorcerer's incantation.

The sky darkened, and the winds swirled. Then, a deep rumble built into a thunderous roar until a great flash came.

Whosoever Pulleth Out this Sword
Hereafter Known by All to be the
Rightful King of England

When the sky returned to normal, a huge marble stone had appeared in the center of the cathedral square. On that marble stone was a giant iron anvil. And thrust deep into the center of the anvil was a great sword.

The blade of the magnificent sword was made of ice-blue steel, and it shone brighter than the sun. The sword's hilt was made of pure gold, carved with ornate patterns more beautiful than those from the finest artisans. It was inlaid with flawless rubies, emeralds, and sapphires.

On the base of the stone were written these words, in bright, gold letters:

Whosoever Pulleth Out this Sword
Is Hereafter Known by All to be the Rightful King of England

When the Archbishop saw what Merlin had created, he could not speak (which was just fine with Merlin—he had to explain what he wanted the Archbishop to do).

"Summon all the nobles in the land," Merlin said. "Call upon the knights and lords to cease their warring, and to come to the square in one month's time—on Christmas Day. Let them come to behold the miracle of the sword, and on that day, to perform the test.

"Whoever can remove the sword is the rightful heir to the throne. When we find that man, then we shall have our king."

The Archbishop nodded that he understood, and Merlin turned to leave.

"When the day comes, your worship," Merlin added, "do not be surprised if those who appear to be noble and worthy of this test fail it miserably; and do not be surprised if one who is among the unknown is the man we seek. For this is not a test for the strong of body—it is a test for the strong of heart and blood."

With that Merlin departed, leaving the Archbishop alone to stare in awe at the sword, and to ponder Merlin's words.

The Great Tournament

Within days, the Archbishop's announcement spread throughout the country. The contest of the sword was to take place in just one month, on Christmas Day.

To make sure that the best of the kingdom's noble subjects would gather, the Archbishop planned a tournament of knights for the three days before the test. This would bring the kingdom together, the Archbishop thought, and unite the people behind the new king.

For now, nobles and knights thought more about winning the crown and the tournament than about conquering their neighbors. For now, the land was calm.

Many miles from the Archbishop's church, a young esquire was very busy. He was polishing his master's armor, and sharpening his swords, and oiling his saddles for battle. He was packing the best tunics and finest robes, and was readying the horses for travel.

Word of the great tournament and the test of the sword had reached the estate on which the young esquire lived, and the young man was very excited. He had just turned eighteen, and was ready to see the world on his own. He had never even left the grounds of the estate, except when he was a young boy—and he did not remember those days well.

But the young esquire was not excited for himself as much as for his stepbrother and master, Sir Kay, who was to take part in the tournament.

"I intend to enter the great tournament of arms, and I need your help," Sir Kay had told the esquire a few days earlier, as he trimmed his beard for the second time that day. (Sir Kay was valiant but a little vain.)

"You will act as my esquire-at-arms. You will help me to emerge victorious from the tournament. And you, Arthur, will carry my spear

and flag onto the battlefield as we claim victory."

Arthur, for that was the young esquire's name, simply nodded and ran off to prepare for the journey. He was glad to have the honor of helping his master win the tournament, and besides, he had never been to London.

Little did he know what wonders lay in store.

The day of the tournament soon arrived. Nearly twenty thousand lords

and ladies had come to see the tournament, and to watch the great test on Christmas Day. They milled about in the velvet-lined stands and watched as the knights entered the courtyard.

Arthur stared in awe at the glittering courtyard as he led Sir Kay and his horse into the jousting arena. This was the knights' procession that paraded all the competitors before the Archbishop and the nobles. The courtyard was covered in rich, velvet canopies of purple and gold.

In the center of the courtyard, under the main canopy, sat the Archbishop himself. He sat where the king would have been seated, if there were a king—on a beautiful velvet throne embroidered in silver and gold.

The Archbishop smiled nervously as the knights and their esquires passed by. He was worried about the test of the sword. Would Merlin's prophesy come true?

Arthur led Sir Kay and his mount to the end of the field where the knights were divided into teams.

The team divisions were made. Sir Kay's team had three fewer knights than the opposing team, but they also had three strong champions. Meantime, the field was cleared, and prepared for the first jousting trial.

The Archbishop stood, blessed the competitors and the onlookers, and waved his hand to signal the start of the tournament. A trumpet fanfare called the knights onto the field.

Arthur watched from the sidelines as Sir Kay's team and the opposing knights rushed forth. The ground rumbled and shook, and the horses galloped into competition.

A great crash and splinter roared through the courtyard when the two teams met, and Arthur winced. Many of the knights were hurt as the horses trampled through. The ground was a mass of broken lances, crushed armor, and dented shields. Knights who were too injured to get up and walk off the field themselves were helped off by their esquires.

Sir Kay did not need Arthur's help, however. He had successfully deflected two lances that were aimed at his chest, and turned around to knock both lance-holders off their steeds. As he galloped through the field, he knocked four more knights off their horses,

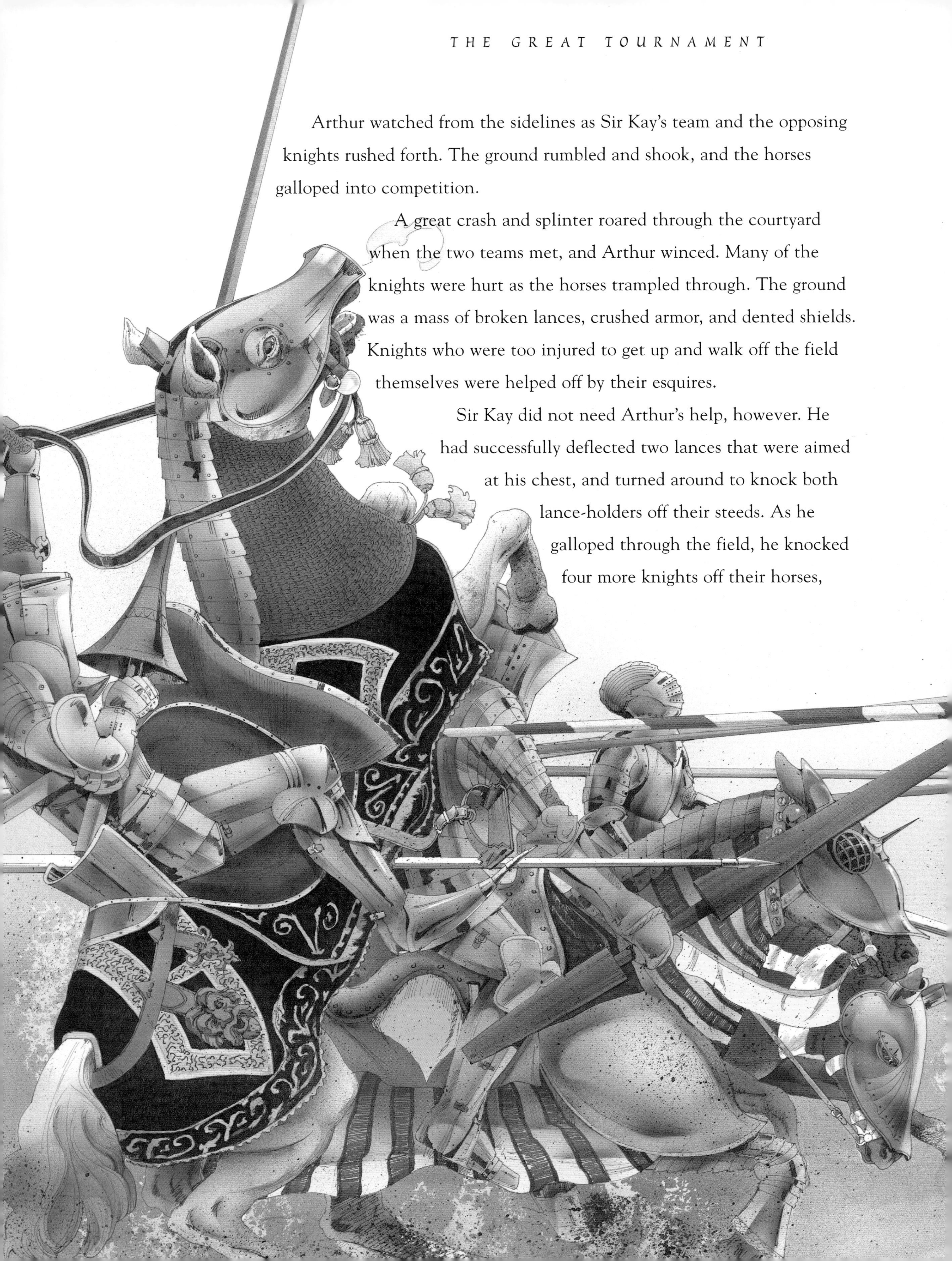

lifting one up into the air with the force of his blow. He was cheered by his team as the most successful competitor.

When the first joust ended, all the remaining knights handed down their lances, and returned to opposite sides of the courtyard. Arthur took Sir Kay's lance, and handed him his heavy broadsword for the second contest.

Again the herald blew his trumpet, and each knight drew his weapon. When they met in the center of the field, the clash and flash of the blades sent rays of blinding sunlight into the onlookers' eyes. And to be sure, if those knights had been longstanding enemies instead of friendly contestants, the wounds inflicted would have been much more serious.

In the middle of the fray, Sir Kay was about to clash with a strong and impressive (and quite large) knight named Sir Balmorgineas. Sir Balmorgineas had been watching Sir Kay throughout the first battle, and knew him to be an able knight. That was just what he wanted; he'd had enough easy fighting that day.

Sir Balmorgineas called him forth, in a booming voice full of challenge and mockery. "Ho! Sir Knight of Naught, come and meet your match!"

Sir Kay grinned underneath his helmet. He was not afraid of the large knight, though he had heard of Sir Balmorgineas' strength. Sir Kay would gladly do battle with him—and gladly defeat him as well.

"I will do battle with thee, Sir Knight of Bombast," said Sir Kay. "And know now that the only match that will be made will be of your face and the ground."

Sir Balmorgineas laughed, and now the helmet hid Sir Kay's red-faced anger. Sir Kay charged towards Sir Balmorgineas, holding his sword high.

The blow Sir Kay dealt was indeed strong, the strongest that Sir Balmorgineas had ever felt. Sir Balmorgineas would have lost consciousness right then and there—if Sir Kay had delivered a second blow quickly, as he meant to do.

But Sir Kay did not strike again—or rather, he could not. His first blow was so fierce that his sword snapped right in two!

Sir Kay had never in his life run from a fight. He was known for his courage, and his pride—but he had to get another sword. There could be no contest without one! So, while Sir Balmorgineas was trying to recover, Sir Kay quickly and quietly left the field.

Arthur came running down to meet him. "Blasted sword, breaks in two in the heat of battle! Why, if I ever get my hands on that blacksmith . . . ," said Sir Kay in frustration.

Arthur, smiling half to reassure Sir Kay and half because he was amused, silenced him. "I will get you another sword, my brother, one worthy of your hands. Rest here until I return. I will be but a moment."

He ran to the edge of the field and leaped over the barrier. As quickly as he could, he ran to the knight's tent where the equipment master would be waiting with replacement swords, shields, and plates of armor.

But when Arthur arrived at the tent, there was no one to be found—everyone was watching the tournament. And the equipment was with them.

Arthur ran out of the tent before he had even decided where to go next. As fast as he could, he ran down a nearby alley, and while he was thinking about where to find a blacksmith, he ran straight into the square of the cathedral, and stopped cold at what he saw.

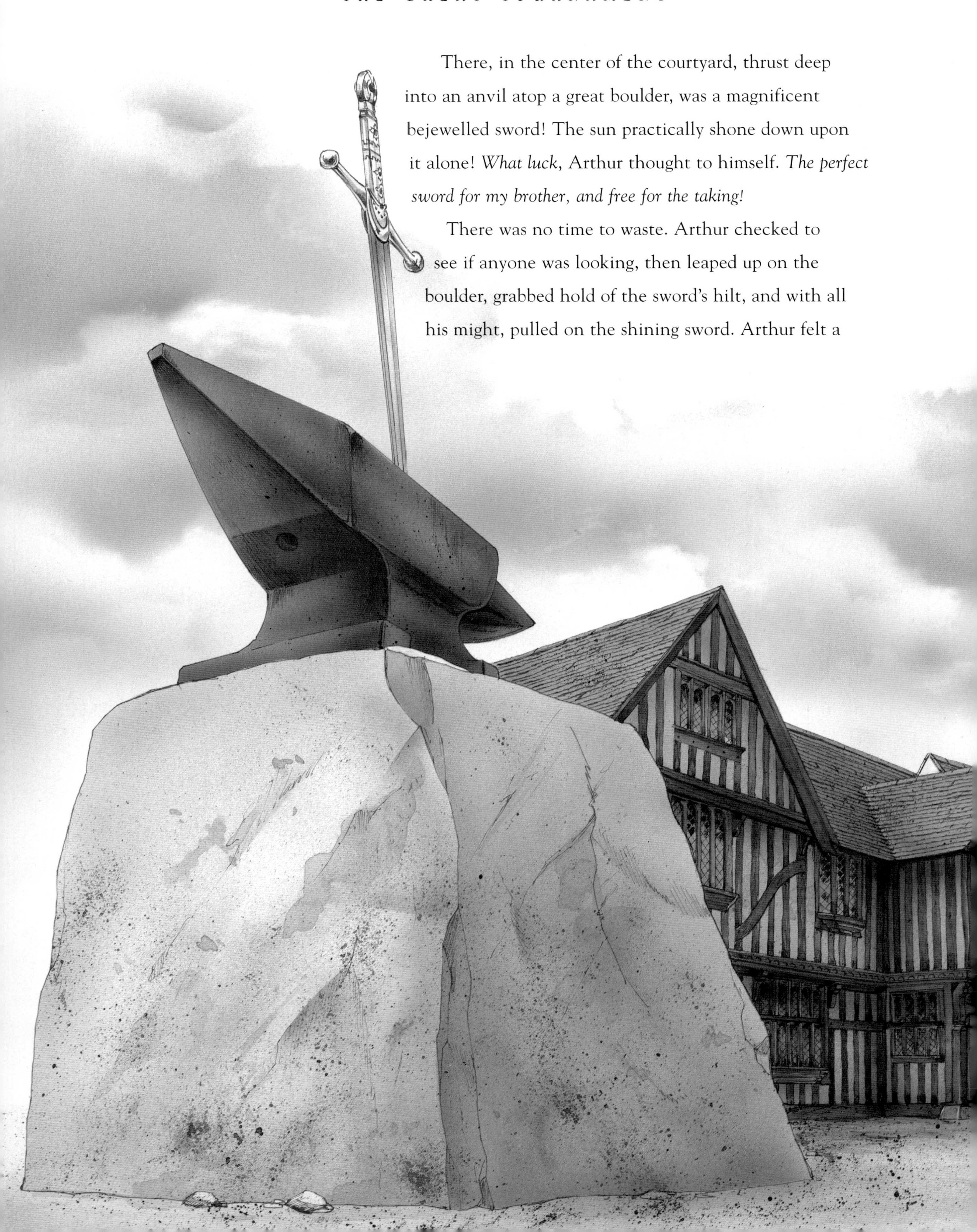

There, in the center of the courtyard, thrust deep into an anvil atop a great boulder, was a magnificent bejewelled sword! The sun practically shone down upon it alone! *What luck*, Arthur thought to himself. *The perfect sword for my brother, and free for the taking!*

There was no time to waste. Arthur checked to see if anyone was looking, then leaped up on the boulder, grabbed hold of the sword's hilt, and with all his might, pulled on the shining sword. Arthur felt a slight shock at first, but much to his surprise, the sword came out quite smoothly, and with hardly any effort!

Arthur quickly removed his cape and wrapped the sword up so that no one would see, jumped down, and ran back to the field of battle. He didn't notice the writing on the other side of the boulder—and he didn't recognize that this was the famous sword that everyone had been talking about. After all, if it were the sword in the contest that was to take place on Christmas Day, surely Arthur would not have been able to remove it!

Sir Kay was grumbling to himself and rattling his armor in frustration when Arthur returned. "Have you found a sword?" he said gruffly.

"Yes, my lord, I did," replied Arthur. He opened his cloak and gave Sir Kay the carefully wrapped sword.

As Sir Kay unwrapped the magnificent sword, his face turned ivory-white. Sir Kay recognized it immediately as the sword from the stone. He couldn't believe that Arthur had removed the true king's sword!

"Wh—where did you get that?" he asked Arthur, his voice cracking slightly.

Arthur, worried that he had done something wrong, told Sir Kay the whole story. "I hope I did not act wrongly," concluded Arthur.

Sir Kay rubbed his chin. "No, no, Arthur," he said, thinking to himself. *It came out easily, he said. Well, then I could have easily removed it myself. I will pretend that I did—and win the crown and all the glory.*

Sir Kay finally said, frowning, "Give the sword and the cloak to me, and go and fetch our father immediately. *Tell no one where the sword came from.*" Then, seeing the dismay on Arthur's face, he smiled an unusually broad smile. "You have done well, Arthur, very well."

This put Arthur a bit more at ease. He was happy to have pleased his master, and did as Sir Kay commanded—although he wondered why Sir Kay had acted so strangely at first. But he did not wonder long. The tournament was beginning again, and Arthur had to find their father, Sir Ector.

So Arthur ran off again, not knowing that the mighty, jewelled sword he had just held in his hands, the great sword he had only moments ago removed from the anvil, was the sword of the future king.

The Miracle of the Sword

Sir Ector, Sir Kay's father and the man who had adopted Arthur, was known for many things—his generosity, his kind nature, and his jovial sense of humor, but above all else, his loud, braying laugh, a laugh that drowned out all of the other sounds around it.

Arthur was very grateful that above the trumpet fanfare, far above the crowd's roar, and farther still above the galloping hooves of the horses on the field, he could hear the boisterous laugh of Sir Ector. This made him very easy to find in the stands.

Arthur made haste to Sir Ector's section and stood in front of him to get his attention. "Sire, Sir Kay has sent me to gather you straightforth. He has left the playing field, and truly, I think something has happened to his head—his face is whiter than snow, and he wears upon it a quizzical look that I have never seen."

Sir Ector became silent for the first time in hours. He could not imagine what would cause his son to leave the field of battle, let alone cause him to call his father from his seat! Immediately, Sir Ector got up.

They soon found Sir Kay, sitting in silence in the middle of the tent. His face had a strange white gleam to it, Sir Ector noticed.

"My son," he said, kneeling down to comfort him, "what is it that ails thee?"

Sir Kay said nothing. He simply smiled a strange smile, took his father by the hand, and led him to a nearby table with a cloak draped over it. Then he turned and spoke to Arthur.

"Will you leave me alone with Father for a while? I need his—his guidance."

Arthur hesitated, then bowed, and went outside the tent. But he was worried about Sir Kay, and a little suspicious, so he lingered outside to hear what he could.

Sir Kay lifted the cloak from the table, and what Sir Ector saw turned him even whiter than his son.

There before him, in shimmering, ruby-clad glory, lay the sword from the stone! Sir Ector knew the sword immediately, and was so surprised to see it that he could find no words on his tongue. He touched the sword gently, and then quickly withdrew his hands and gulped.

"Where—where did you get this?" asked Sir Ector.

"I broke my sword in the second contest on the field," said Sir Kay, purposely staring away from his father's questioning eyes. "And I found this sword to use instead. I hope I did no wrong by removing it from the anvil atop the stone?"

Sir Ector did not know what to think. "If indeed you removed the sword from the stone, my son, then you are the rightful King of Britain. The stone itself tells us this." Sir Ector spoke hesitantly, as if he felt that something were wrong, and Sir Kay widened his eyes, pretending to be surprised at the news.

"But if you did withdraw the great sword, then you should be able to thrust it back again just as easily," Sir Ector continued. *It's not that I don't trust my son*, Sir Ector told himself. *It's just that this is all a little hard to believe.*

Sir Kay shot his eyes forward, and blurted out, "Who could do such a thing as that? Who in this land could perform a miracle and thrust a sword into solid iron?"

His father noticed the excitement and fear in Sir Kay's voice, and knew he was onto something. "Yes, indeed it would be a great miracle. But no greater a miracle than you have performed by removing it. After all, who could imagine a man able to withdraw a sword from solid iron and not able to thrust it back?"

Now Sir Kay could find no words on *his* tongue. He had been caught. *How can I perform that miracle*, he thought. *No one can! And yet, if I want to be king, I must replace the sword.* Then, in an instant, he knew the answer. *If Arthur could remove the sword, then surely I can put it back. After all, Arthur is much weaker than I.*

"Very well, Father," said Sir Kay, slightly irritated, "I will repeat the miracle." He wrapped up the sword, left the tent, and went with Sir Ector to the courtyard to prove he was worthy of the crown.

As they left the tent, Arthur ducked around the corner to avoid being seen. He had heard everything. *How could Sir Kay betray me so cruelly?* he thought.

Angry and confused, Arthur followed behind as they made their way to the courtyard. He made sure that they did not see him, and hid once they reached the cathedral.

Upon arriving at the courtyard, Sir Kay surveyed the scene. He circled the great stone several times, and even climbed on top of it to see if the sword had left a mark on the anvil where it had been. There was no mark—the anvil was as clean and solid as if it had been forged that very afternoon.

The anvil was much larger than Sir Kay remembered, and he began to lose confidence. *What is this my father asks me to do?* he thought to himself, *What man is there that could thrust a sword into this solid block of iron?* But he remembered that somehow, Arthur had removed the great sword—and if Arthur could do it, so could he.

At last, Sir Kay raised the sword over his head, ready to plunge it into the heart of the anvil. *If Arthur could do it, so can I, if Arthur could do it, so can I, if Arthur could do it, so can I . . .* thought Sir Kay.

The words swirled around and around in his head as he gathered his strength, took a deep breath, and with all his might, brought the sword down—thrusting it through the iron, straight into the center of the anvil!

At least, that was what Sir Kay expected to happen. What actually occurred was this: In a flash, the sword came down through the air, and with a loud CLANG! the sword hit the anvil and skidded off the edge. It did not slice through to the center of the anvil, or even pierce the iron. It didn't even leave a scratch!

Sir Kay, amazed to see the anvil as clean as before, gathered his strength and tried again. Nothing. He tried again—nothing. And again—nothing. And yet again—still nothing. At last, defeated and out of breath, Sir Kay stepped down from the stone.

"Father, no man alive could perform this miracle," he said, wiping the sweat from his brow.

Sir Ector shook his head. "Then how could you have removed it?"

Before Sir Kay could answer, Arthur stepped from the bushes.

"I wonder if *I* might try," he said, staring straight at Sir Kay.

Sir Ector was taken aback. "By what authority would you claim to handle the great sword, Arthur? You are but an esquire."

"Because it was I who removed it in the first place. So, I should be able to put it back." He took the sword from Sir Kay's hands. "May I, *brother*?" Arthur asked, his voice dripping with sarcasm. He was furious and this was very unlike Arthur. He was usually so calm and considerate.

Sir Ector had an odd look in his eyes, as if he knew something. Arthur broke his angry glare to notice this. "Father, why do you look so strangely upon me? Are you angry with me?" he asked.

Sir Ector replied, "Angry, no. Most certainly no. If you wish to try the sword, you have my blessing, for what it is worth."

Arthur climbed to the top of the stone. He took the sword in one hand, placed the tip against the center of the anvil, and slowly pressed down.

Nothing happened at first. Then there came a quiet hiss, like steam rising from cobblestones after a rainstorm. And the sword began to smoothly slide down.

When it was in about halfway to the hilt, Arthur stopped pressing and removed his hand. He breathed a sigh of relief, and stepped down confidently.

He saw Sir Ector kneeling on the cobblestone, his head bowed. Arthur cried out to him, "Why do you kneel before me? You, who have cared for me since you adopted me many years ago?"

"My lord," cried Sir Ector, "I kneel because I can clearly see now that you are not a mere esquire. The blood of kings flows through your veins."

"What do you mean?" asked Arthur, not believing his ears. Sir Ector pointed to the words written on the other side of the stone.

Arthur circled the great boulder, and read the words Merlin had branded into the stone. *I am to be king?* he thought. *How is this possible? I knew Sir Ector adopted me in my youth, but from royalty?*

"I don't understand, Father," he said. Sir Kay watched silently as Sir Ector explained.

"The time has come for you to know, Arthur. Eighteen years ago, in the middle of a dark winter's night, a man came to my door. He was tall and ancient, draped in an enchanter's cloak, and he wore the king's signet ring. He introduced himself as one of King Uther-Pendragon's advisors, and told me that he had a special task for me.

Whosoever Out
is Hereafter
Rightful King of

"I was to meet him at midnight the following night, at the outskirts of Uther-Pendragon's castle—and to tell no one.

"The next night, when Kay was asleep, I went to the meeting place. The man was waiting. He introduced himself as Merlin, the king's enchanter. In his arms he held a small covered basket—and the basket seemed to move on its own every so often.

"Merlin lifted the cloak to show me the basket's contents. Inside was a baby, not much more than six months of age. I could not take my eyes from him. His eyes were piercingly blue, and his face was strong and calming. Arthur, you were that child.

"Merlin told me to take you and to raise you from that day on. You were in great danger, he said, and I was able to keep you from it. He told me nothing more, and said that I shouldn't ask—he said nothing of your birth, or of the sort of danger you were in. Only that no one was to know where you had come from.

"I swore that I would take care, and keep your secret, and from that day on I have been your father. But now it is clear from whose blood you came. Your father was Uther-Pendragon himself—for who but the true son of the king could draw forth the sword from the stone?"

Arthur was in quiet tears by the end of the story. He helped Sir Ector up.

Sir Kay finally kneeled, and spoke. "Forgive me, my lord, for betraying you! I beg your forgiveness." Sir Kay bowed his head in shame.

"I cannot hold a grudge against you, my brother. For though you have acted thoughtlessly today, you have treated me like a brother for years. But I feel—I—" Arthur stopped, and broke down into tears.

"Why do you cry, my lord?" asked Sir Ector.

"I feel as if my life up to now has been a lie. I know not who I am," said Arthur.

"You are Arthur, son of Uther-Pendragon," said a voice from the bushes. "And you have come just in time." Arthur looked up, and out walked a majestically tall, willowy man in a sorcerer's cloak. He seemed to glide over the cobblestones as he moved towards them. It was clear that this was the man who had come to Sir Ector's house so many years ago—Merlin, the enchanter.

Merlin creased his ancient gray brow. "What is all this weeping? This is a time for cheer! We have a new king!" He turned to Sir Ector.

"You have served the kingdom well, Sir Ector. In Arthur lies the hope of Britain, and you have raised him well." He turned to Arthur, and placed his arm around his shoulder.

"And you, young prince, I have been watching you all morning through an enchanted mirror. I saw how you withdrew the sword, and how you replaced it again.

"And I saw, too, beyond this morning. I saw how you will rule with grace and dignity, and how you will make peace in the kingdom, surrounding yourself with loyal knights. Many adventures are to come for you, my lord, after you restore the kingdom to harmony again."

Now Merlin spoke to all of them. "But we must keep these events quiet until Christmas Day," said Merlin. "Then Arthur can claim the kingship before the eyes of all the realm. We must keep him safe until then—for in Arthur alone is our hope."

Sir Kay and Sir Ector swore that they would keep him safe, and Arthur swore that he would keep silent about what had happened.

Merlin bowed to the man who was soon to be king, and left. Arm in arm, Arthur, Sir Kay, and Sir Ector left the courtyard after him.

Back in the courtyard, the sword glistened, waiting for Christmas Day.

The Day of the Contest

Christmas day always brought hundreds of people to the Archbishop's cathedral. They came every year for the mass, and to greet their friends and neighbors on this festive occasion.

But this Christmas day brought with it not merely a glorious sun, a light dusting of snow, and the usual churchgoers. This Christmas brought many thousands of people to fill the courtyard and its outskirts—and they weren't there for the Archbishop's notoriously long sermon.

Today was the day of the great test of the sword. People from all over the kingdom, from all walks of life—knights and nobles, shopkeepers and farmers—all had come to try to remove the sword from the anvil, and to claim the throne as their own.

The Archbishop sat on a raised throne right next to the anvil, underneath a canopy of royal velvet. He was to preside over the contest. He wanted to be sure that nothing went wrong.

The contestants were lined up in order of their class. First in line were the kings from other nations—nineteen kings and sixteen dukes had travelled there from all over the world, each hoping to claim the crown. Next were the knights and nobles of lower order, and then the commoners—the merchants, farmers, and peasants. Arthur, Sir Ector, Sir Kay, and Merlin were at the end of the line, disguised in peasant cloaks.

At nine o'clock sharp, the Archbishop rose. He raised his hands to silence the restless crowd. He had prepared a long speech to welcome the contestants and bless the ceremony. This was surely the largest crowd he had ever addressed.

"People! Loyal subjects! Worthy travellers! I would have your attention," he spoke. But the crowd paid no attention, talking among themselves even louder than they had before.

"All who have come for the test of the sword, give me your ears! I have prepared a speech—" the Archbishop pleaded at the top of his voice.

King Lot of Orkney, who was first in line, spoke for the crowd. "With all due respect, Archbishop, we want the contest to begin. Many of us have travelled far and wide to come here. We know you have worked hard for this day—but so have we. And now we want to be put to the test." The crowd cheered loudly in agreement.

The Archbishop was a bit hurt and insulted, but he understood how they felt. He merely bowed his head, waved his hand, and took his seat. "Very well," he said reluctantly, "Let the test begin."

King Lot mounted the boulder and took the sword by the hilt. He saluted the Archbishop, then saluted his entourage confidently. He bent his body forward, and with all his might, pulled up on the sword.

The sword did not move, though the king strained till he was red in the face. He tried a second time and pulled harder. His face only became redder. Finally, with the crowd yelling at him to step aside and to let another try, he pulled a third time.

There was a great CRRRAAACK! The sword remained in the stone—but the king had dislocated his shoulder.

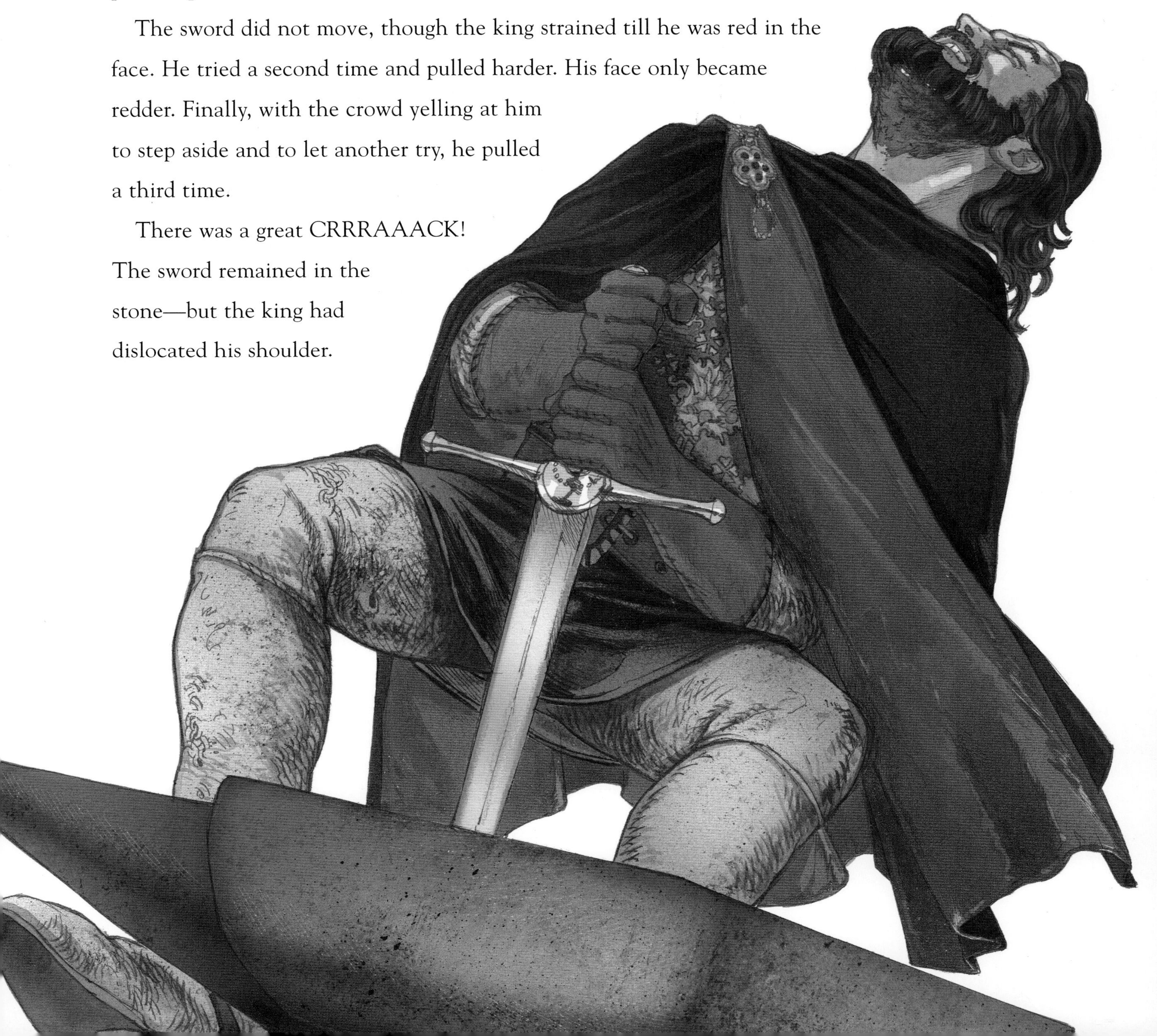

Embarrassed, and in quite a bit of pain, the king was carried from the stone by his esquires. The crowd laughed. "One kingdom is enough for him," someone shouted. And the contest went on.

The remaining kings in line did not fare much better than King Lot. King Fion of Scotland tried to remove the blade, but could not. King Mark of Cornwall went next, and after him his brother-in-law, the King of North Wales, and after him King Ryence of Gore—but they too failed. And so it went, as all the kings and all the dukes tried their best to remove the sword. No one did any better than anyone else—unless you count the fact that no other noble or king strained themselves as badly as King Lot.

Many people in the crowd were astonished that the kings and dukes had failed. "If kings and dukes of high estate and noble blood have failed, how can we hope to win?" they said.

The kings and nobles agreed. They circled angrily around the Archbishop to protest.

"This unfair test was made to bring us shame and embarrassment," said King Ryence.

The crowd cheered, and Arthur excitedly swung the sword over his head so that it flashed in the sunlight like lightning.

Then, Arthur held the sword aloft in one hand and set the point of the sword back upon the anvil. He pressed upon it lightly, and the sword slid smoothly back in place.

The crowd cheered more loudly than they had ever cheered at any jousting match. Before their very eyes a miracle had taken place.

"Long live the new king! Long live King Arthur!" the people cried.

Arthur smiled wide, and his eyes sparkled. He was so caught up in the joy of the moment that he removed and replaced the sword three more times—each one a little more enthusiastically than the time before.

Even the kings and dukes, who were angry when Arthur first performed the miracle of the sword, were cheering by the end. For though this meant that they would not be chosen, they could see that there was more to this young man than met the eye. They could see that he was truly of royal blood, and they wanted him on their side when he was crowned king.

Standing before the crowd, Arthur easily commanded the attention and respect of all his subjects. He suddenly seemed far older than his eighteen years. Even Merlin was struck by Arthur's presence. Gazing upon the future king, Merlin envisioned his reign. The young

prince would become the most famous king that ever lived in Britain, and the many years of his reign would bring wondrous occasions and grand quests. He would rule with grace and dignity, surround himself with loyal knights, and bring peace to the realm. The future of the kingdom was at long last secure.

The Archbishop stood before Arthur and again addressed the crowd. "Lords, ladies, and good people of this land, I am satisfied by what I've seen. This young man has performed the miracle that each of you in your turn has failed to perform, and I proudly accept him as my king." The crowd roared its approval as the Archbishop knelt before Arthur.

Arthur simply smiled at those who were soon to be his subjects. What words could express the vast joy within his heart? And as they lifted him off the stone and carried him through the streets in celebration, Arthur's spirits soared. Indeed, his blue eyes seemed to meet the very sky which they held inside. At that moment, his heart was overflowing with joy.

He was no longer Arthur, esquire-at-arms. He was Arthur, King of Britain.

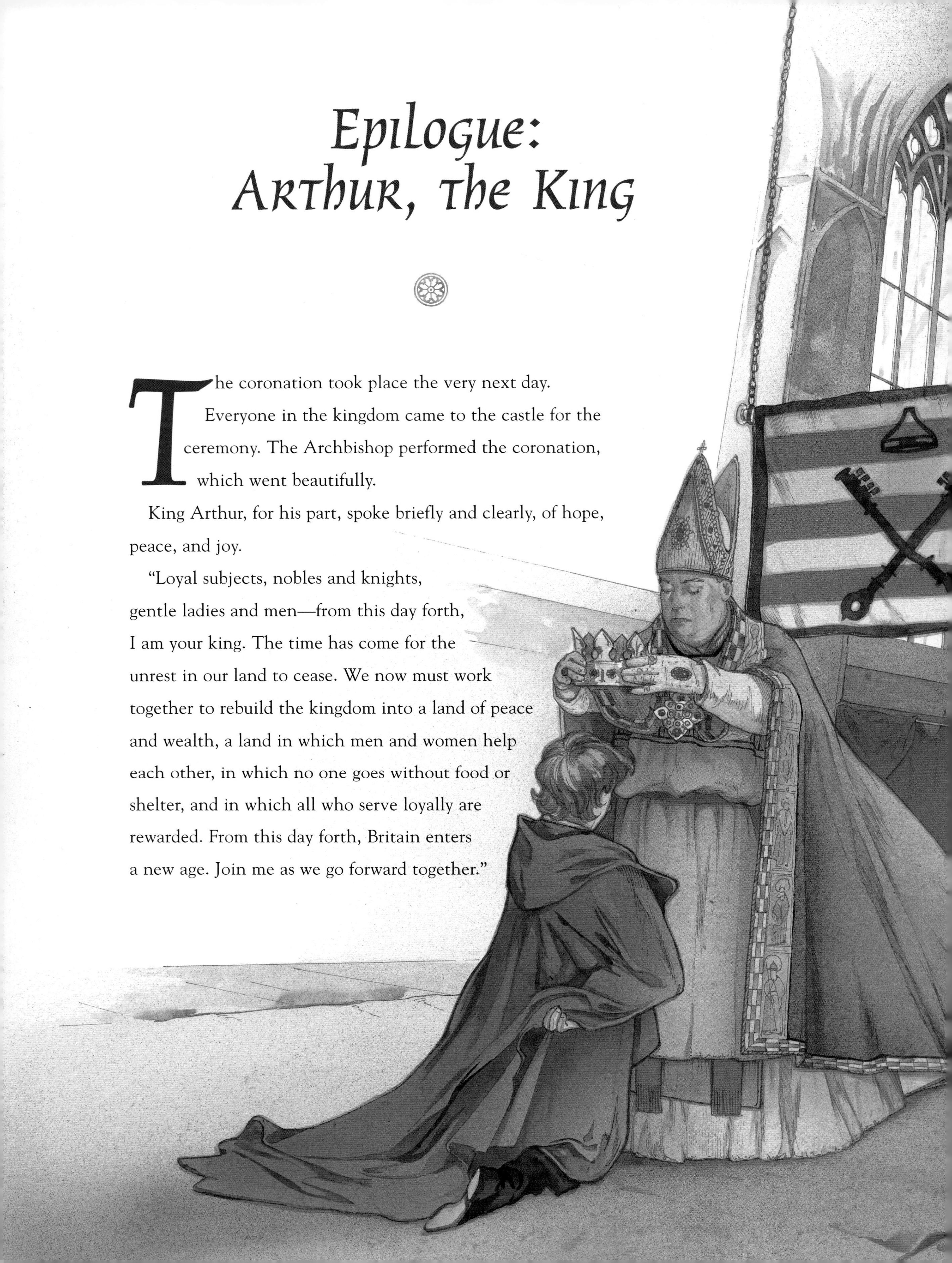

Epilogue: Arthur, the King

The coronation took place the very next day. Everyone in the kingdom came to the castle for the ceremony. The Archbishop performed the coronation, which went beautifully.

King Arthur, for his part, spoke briefly and clearly, of hope, peace, and joy.

"Loyal subjects, nobles and knights, gentle ladies and men—from this day forth, I am your king. The time has come for the unrest in our land to cease. We now must work together to rebuild the kingdom into a land of peace and wealth, a land in which men and women help each other, in which no one goes without food or shelter, and in which all who serve loyally are rewarded. From this day forth, Britain enters a new age. Join me as we go forward together."

And they did. King Arthur was immediately loved and accepted by his subjects, who respected his decisions in the many years of his reign to come.

Merlin became his royal enchanter and closest advisor. Arthur appointed Sir Kay as prime minister, showing that he held no grudge, and Sir Ector also served in the royal cabinet.

King Arthur's greatness was known throughout the world, and noble souls and great knights came to Britain to undertake many wondrous adventures with the renowned king.

But those are other stories. When Arthur was crowned, it was more than enough that Britain once again had a king—and that the kingdom was once again at peace.